THREE
SCARY
STORIES

For my brother, Nicholas

THREE
SCARY
STORIES

FRIEDA HUGHES
Illustrated by CHRIS RIDDELL

Collins
An imprint of HarperCollinsPublishers

First published in Great Britain by Collins in 2001

Collins is an imprint of HarperCollins*Publishers* Ltd,
77-85 Fulham Palace Road, Hammersmith,
London W6 8JB

The HarperCollins website address is
www.**fire**and**water**.com

3 5 7 9 8 6 4 2

Copyright © Frieda Hughes 2001
Illustrations by Chris Riddell

The author asserts the moral right to be
identified as the author of the work.

ISBN 0 00 710601 7

Printed and bound in Great Britain by
Omnia Books Limited, Glasgow

Contents

Little Brother

Big sisters are supposed to look after their little brothers. But little brothers have snotty noses, can't tie their own shoelaces, play computer games with the volume at full blast, and think it's really funny to collect spiders and then forget to feed them.

My brother Nick is a scientist. I'd call him strange. He's only eleven, but he knows the degree of all the facets that make up a perfect diamond. He's not into computer games, but he does collect insects. Every now and then I sneak into his bedroom to see what he's got in his jars and his little row of fish tanks.

For a while he tried to breed axolotls, those prehistoric lizard things that live under water, and have gills like seaweed. Then he discovered his six axolotls were all male. How unlucky can you get?

He kept rats for a while, too, so he could feed the babies to the axolotls, but they bred far too easily and Mum made him give them to the pet shop. At one point there were eighty-six of them — they filled every fish tank he had. But they ate each other because the axolotls couldn't eat them fast enough.

Now he's trying to make a birthday present for Dad. Dad likes flowers and he's always entering them in competitions. But he never wins, so Nick is determined to come up with something that will make things grow. For an eleven-year-old, he's quite brilliant, really.

I hadn't managed to save enough pocket money to buy Dad a present, so I spent ages walking up and down the beach near us, looking for that special rock that I could call a paperweight. I found a big, smooth, oval one with orange streaks in it, took it home, varnished it so the colours would always show up as though the stone was wet, and glued a piece of felt to the bottom of it, so it wouldn't scratch Dad's desk. I felt pretty pleased with myself.

* * * *

This morning, I sneaked into Nick's bedroom while he was washing before school. He had a row of plant pots on one of his shelves, and in each one was a green sprout. On his work table in the corner, where he keeps all his concoctions and bottles and test tubes, was a little row of jars, each labelled with a series of letters, like a code.

"What are you doing in here, Sarah?" he demanded angrily. I hadn't noticed him come in behind me. He started to push me out of his room.

"I don't go snooping round YOUR room," he complained.

"I just wanted to see how you were getting on with Dad's birthday present," I explained. "His birthday is in just over two weeks. Think you'll be able to cook up something for him by then?"

Nick scowled at me and slammed the door.

* * * *

Two days later, I was getting my slippers from under my bed, when an enormous wolf spider scuttled out — you know, the spiders that grow huge, and live in holes like mice. I don't normally scream. Really, I don't, but I know that these spiders can give you a nasty nip.

So I screamed. Nick came running, so did Mum and Dad, but they don't like spiders any more than I do. So there I was, standing on my bed, Mum and Dad peering in from the doorway, and Nick, crawling up to the spider on his hands and knees with a jam jar.

The spider hesitated for a second, and that was all the time Nick needed. Quick as a flash, he had the spider under the jar. He slipped a piece of card beneath the jar to seal it off.

"I'm going to call him Goliath," he announced.

****

By the following Friday, Nick's little plants were all sprouting tomatoes. "I don't just want them to grow big," Nick explained, "I want them to taste wonderful. But I can't try them out until I know it's safe, so I need a couple of guinea-pigs to test them on first, just to make sure I won't be sick if I eat them."

Even though Nick had planted them at the same time, each plant was at a different stage. Standing in a row, it was obvious that each one was bigger than the last. Except for the two at the end, which looked dead.

I picked up one of the last pots. In it lay a

brown, soggy mess like celery that had been left at the bottom of the fridge to rot.

"It's because each pot has had a bigger dose of my special concoction than the one before," said Nick. "But it seems to reach a point where the plant can't take it, and the growth mixture acts like a poison. Just like in real medicine — too much of something can kill you."

"So why don't you throw it away?" I asked him.

He just grinned.

"So what's in your 'special invention'?" I wanted to know.

He grinned again.

"Can't tell you," he said, secretively, "but I'm going to call it XR28, because this is my twenty-eighth try."

"Very catchy," I told him.

"I thought so," he replied, already preoccupied. Then I noticed the spider, crouching at the bottom of a specimen jar, feeling the slipperiness of the sides with its long forelegs.

"*Ugh*," I gasped, "you've still got that horrible thing! What are you going to do with it?"

"You mean Goliath? I'll feed him, when I have time to catch a few flies…" he muttered, pouring something out of one of his bottles into another.

I picked off a piece of rotting plant from the pot I was holding, and threw it into the top of the spider's open jar. Not a big enough piece for the spider to be able to climb out of his prison, but enough for him to take notice.

"Nick!" I called. "Look at this!" The spider was crawling over the plant and devouring it.

"You shouldn't have done that," Nick told me ominously. "The stuff I've been feeding the plant on will probably kill him, because it's so concentrated."

"But it could make him grow, couldn't it?" I asked.

"No," replied Nick. "The molecular structure of the plant feed is specifically mixed to address the genetic structure of a plant, not an insect. At least, I think so…"

I know I must have looked surprised. There was my little brother, eleven years old and not very tall, talking as if he knew what he meant. At least, he sounded pretty convincing to me.

That week, Nick spent all his pocket money on buying two baby rabbits – the pet shop had sold out of guinea pigs. He kept them in a hutch in his room. I thought they were adorable, both grey and soft, with ears that drooped down the sides of their faces, but Nick wouldn't let me touch them.

"They're just to test my tomato plants on," he insisted. "You can't play with things which are part of my experiment, you might ruin it."

I looked in on the rabbits two days later. They looked happy and plump. Then I noticed the plants. The dead ones had begun to dry up and shrivel into crumpled black twigs, but the others were growing enormous, each one a little larger than the one next to it.

That's when I saw the spider again. He was still in his tall glass jar, but there was no rotting bit of tomato plant in there with him, Nick must have cleared it out — or maybe Goliath devoured the whole lot? He looked shrunken and half dead. I bent down and studied him closely. Two big eyes and lots of little ones, peered back at me unnervingly.

I started to search for something to give him to eat. I might have hated Goliath, but I couldn't bear to think of him starving to death. I would have carried him out to the garden and let him go, if only I'd been able to touch the jar... But that was out of the question, I might drop it and Goliath might escape, crawling over my feet or up my leg. *Ugh*!

All I could find was a dead fly lying on the windowsill. I picked it up by one wing and dropped it into Goliath's jar, but he wasn't very interested. He hooked the fly with one of the spiky, sticky ends of his feet, and dangled it in the air for a moment. It was all dried up from being in the sun.

Then Goliath dropped it and curled his long legs under his body again, the way spiders do when they're dying.

I went to find Nick to tell him his spider was hungry, but he didn't seem to be anywhere in the house. I found some mince meat in the fridge, waiting to become spaghetti bolognaise, and put a little bit in Goliath's jar. He seemed to sniff the meat, like a dog might. Then his two front legs unfolded and crammed it into his mouth.

He was really starving; I threw several bits of meat into the jar, and he ate them all. Then I noticed his belly was swelling, it looked tight and uncomfortable.

With a feeling of horror, I saw the top of his belly-sack begin to pull apart, like a too-tight tee-shirt that was about to split. I ran for the door. I hoped Nick wouldn't realise what I'd done when he found his new pet all burst open in the bottom of the jar.

****

Funnily enough, Nick never mentioned it. But he started to spend even more time in his room which made it difficult for me to check on Goliath's well-being.

When I asked him how Goliath was, he just shrugged and said 'fine', and disappeared back into his room, slamming the door behind him.

"How about the XR28?" I called after him, knocking on the door and trying to open it. But he'd jammed a chair under the handle on the other side.

"XR28 is doing fine," he yelled back. "I'm just having a little problem with the flavour — the tomatoes have no flavour yet."

"Neither do the ones at the supermarket," I shouted. "Most of them aren't ripened in the sun like they used to be."

I could hear Nick muttering to himself. "Sun… mmmm. Natural light. Humph."

"Hey, Nick!" I called through the door again. "Have you made sure it's OK to eat those tomatoes after the gunk you've been feeding them?"

"I tested it on the rabbits first," he replied, "and they're fine – they're still alive!"

****

When we were getting ready for school the next day, I left my homework on my bed on purpose, so I had an excuse to go back for it.

Half-way down the road I told my brother.

"I'll come with you," said Nick obligingly. But I told him I could run faster than him and I'd be quicker if I was on my own.

Mum was surprised to see me back again. "Be quick!" she shouted after me, as I raced upstairs.

I grabbed my homework off the bed, then sneaked into Nick's room. Goliath was still there in his otherwise empty jar, legs curled up again. I

pulled the little plastic bag I was carrying out of my pocket, and gave him some fresh flies I'd found, and a little bit of chopped-up meat.

"HURRY UP!" Mum cried. Quickly, I emptied the rest of the meat from the little bag, into the jar. For a split second Goliath sat there, looking almost stunned. Then he began to gobble it all up fast. I couldn't stay to watch, but at least the food would keep him going for a while. I glanced across the room at the rabbits — they looked quite happy. They were larger than I'd remembered, but I knew that baby rabbits grow quickly.

★ ★ ★ ★

Nick stormed into my room later that night. "DID YOU FEED MY SPIDER?" he demanded. Sheepishly, I nodded. He grabbed my arm and dragged me to his room.

Nick stood me in front of his work table. "What exactly did you do to Goliath?" he asked.

"I gave him some meat," I told him. "He was

starving." I peered into the spider jar to get a closer look at the tangle of legs at the bottom. Nick put his hand in and pulled out a lifeless, black, leggy body.

"Oh, it's all right," he snapped, as I shrank away from it, "Goliath isn't actually here, this is just what's left of him."

I stared and stared at the thing he was holding up in front of my face. It sure looked like the spider to me.

"It's just his skin," Nick explained, seeing my puzzled expression. "What I want to know is, where's the rest of him?"

Suddenly, I felt very faint and had to sit on the bed. "What do you mean, 'where is the rest of him'?" I asked nervously.

"I mean, that if you look at the legs of this thing," he said, holding it up to my face for an even closer look, "you can see they're hollow. The real legs aren't there any more," he said sharply. "As for the body sack, it's as empty as an old cushion cover. Goliath must have got big enough to reach the top of his jar and climbed out, leaving his old skin behind."

"So the spider's in here, somewhere?" I said, looking around the room.

"Only if you shut the door after you left this morning," Nick replied.

I was sure I had. Wasn't I? Impatiently, Nick fell to his knees on the floor and started looking under the bed. I swung my feet up and tucked them beneath me.

Systematically, Nick began to search every inch of the room, but without success. Until he got to the window seat. Underneath it, he found a dead mouse. It was dry and empty like a shell, as if its insides had been sucked out.

"We have to find Goliath," Nick told me. "If Mum or Dad do, they'll only kill him, and I want to study him some more."

"Why did he grow suddenly?" I asked. I had this horrible feeling that I already knew the answer.

"The XR28-soaked tomato plant," Nick replied. "When you threw it into the jar, instead of killing Goliath, it infected him with the propensity to grow when fed. That's why I wasn't feeding him, dummy!"

"Propensity?" I repeated.

"It just means that now he can't eat without growing huge very quickly," replied Nick. "The rabbits haven't had very much of the stuff, because they haven't eaten any of the plants with the greatest concentration in, so they should be all right."

"And which of the plants did *you* try?" I asked Nick. He looked away for a moment.

"Only a tiny bit of the first one, to see what the flavour was like, that's all. I should be OK," he added confidently.

Suddenly, there was a loud wail from the kitchen. "*Ni-ick!*" It was my mother. Nick and I hurtled down the stairs.

There, in the open doorway between the

kitchen and the back garden, lay the bitten-off head of a small bird.

Without batting an eyelid, Nick tossed the little bird's head to the back of the yard, where one of the neighbourhood cats would be bound to find it.

"Did you go into my room today, Mum?" he asked, casually.

"Of course, Nick, I vacuumed upstairs after Sarah came back for her homework," said Mum.

There, I knew I hadn't been the one to leave the door open.

Then Mum made Nick wash his hands really well after touching the dead bird's head. As for me? I checked my room really thoroughly, then firmly shut the door.

* * * *

It was Nick who woke me up the next morning.

"Sarah, *Sarah*!" he whispered hoarsely in my ear.

"What is it?" I mumbled, rubbing my eyes.

"Come quick, come and have a look!" he demanded, pulling my duvet off me.

Bleary-eyed, I followed him. There, all lined up as before, were his plant pots. Except that now, all the tomato plants had been chewed away, right down to the earth, even the dead ones.

"What happened?" I gasped.

"I know it sounds crazy, but I think Goliath came back for some more XR28," said Nick. "I hadn't made up any more of my mixture, so he ate all the plants instead."

I saw the window was wide open — it had been a warm night last night. Then I noticed the rabbit hutch had what appeared to be teeth marks on it, but the rabbits seemed OK. I suggested we move them into my room, and Nick agreed.

Then we sat on the edge of his bed, trying to imagine how big Goliath might be and how we could explain to Mum and Dad what had happened. Or one of the teachers from school. Or a policeman. Or someone from the Government...

"They'll all want to know how I did it," sighed Nick despondently.

"Then I suppose you'll have to give them your secret mixture," I told him. But it all seemed pretty undesirable — the idea of everyone questioning us and wanting to know every little detail.

"We'll just have to try and catch Goliath ourselves," Nick told me decisively.

And I reluctantly had to agree.

"Then we'll have to kill him," I added.

Nick didn't comment.

★★★★

"I'll make more XR28, to tempt him back," said Nick, the next day. "He should be able to sniff it out. And I've made a really delicious, sweet-tasting sleeping potion. Insects love it, so Goliath certainly should – it'll knock him out."

"*Then* what do we do?" I asked. "Drop a brick on him? Yuk! Think of the mess!"

"No, we'll just find a jar big enough to put over him," Nick told me calmly. But what we actually ended up with was the big plastic dustbin from the kitchen…

* * * *

That night, we waited until Mum and Dad had gone to bed. Then, we lifted the bag of rubbish out of the dustbin and took the bin to Nick's room. He had made up a new batch of XR28, and dabbed some on the windowsill, leaving the window open just like the night before.

Then Nick poured a bit of the XR28 and the sleeping potion into a bowl; he'd mixed the sleeping potion with some apple juice in the apple juice carton.

"*Apple* juice?" I asked curiously.

"Oh, it's not an important ingredient," Nick

replied. "I only use it to mix my sleeping potion in. It masks the flavour, and like I said, insects love it because it's sweet and sticky."

"Did you leave the carton in the kitchen earlier tonight?" I demanded, grasping Nick's arm.

Nick nodded, puzzled.

"Oh no, Mum and Dad each took a glass of apple juice to bed with them!" I told him. "We have to stop them drinking it!"

Nick turned and ran to their bedroom. He came back with a dejected look on his face. "It's too late," he murmured.

I went to check on Mum and Dad myself. They were sleeping soundly, and when I called gently to them, they didn't stir. The glasses that had held the apple juice were empty by their bedsides.

Then I tried to wake Mum by shaking her shoulder, but she just let out an unladylike snort, and rolled over. I hurried back to Nick.

We decided to stage a night vigil. We each took a torch – Nick hid his in bed with him, and was still wearing his clothes. I sat in a chair by the door, also fully dressed. I didn't want to let on to Nick just how scared I was, but I kept glancing at the door handle to make sure that I could still tell exactly where it was, in the moonlight that shone into the room.

In case we fell asleep, we'd placed a pile of old tin cans that Mum had been collecting for the recycling bins, in front of the window. Goliath was bound to disturb them if he came in.

****

Time passed very slowly. "*Nick, are you awake?*" I whispered, after what seemed like hours.

"*Yes,*" he replied. I could tell his voice was still alert.

Some time later, I asked again. This time his voice sounded rather strained and tired.

I didn't ask a third time because I fell asleep myself.

As dawn broke, I yawned and stretched my stiff limbs. My neck ached a bit. When I opened my eyes I found that Nick wasn't in bed and his bedclothes were strewn across the floor towards the window. Why hadn't I heard anything? Why hadn't the tin cans been disturbed?

I looked for the new bottle of XR28, but it had gone, and there were pincer marks in the windowsill — so strong that they had splintered the wood! The bowl of XR28 and apple-juice sleeping draught was empty.

I glanced at the clock beside Nick's bed and saw it was only four-thirty, but the birds were singing already, even though it was still very grey outside.

I stuck my head out of the window. "*Nick!*" I whispered hoarsely, trying not to wake anyone. But there was no answer, just an eerie stillness. Then a crow lurched from the apple tree at the bottom of the garden, with a disgruntled croak.

I found Nick's torch under the pillows on his bed where he'd left it. Did this mean Nick had been taken? I was sure he wouldn't have left it behind otherwise. But how could it all happen so quietly? I scoured the bedroom, looking for signs. Nothing.

In exasperation, I flung myself down on the bed. Then I saw them. There, on the ceiling, were scratchy smudges. Dirty spider footprints. My blood ran cold. The thing had walked right over where I'd been sleeping in the chair.

I leapt off the bed, ran downstairs and unlocked the back door to the garden. First, I looked back up at Nick's window, to see if there were any footmarks which might show me exactly where the spider had climbed down the side of the house. But there was nothing.

As I stood in the misty morning stillness, thinking, something rattled in the gutter above me. I looked up, but couldn't see anything. Then there was a second rattle, like a pebble rolling down the roof tiles. I walked all round the house, peering up in the grey morning light, trying to see the top of the roof. Then, there by the chimney, I saw a huddled bundle.

Straining to see, I tried to make out what it was, but without success. However, there was one way to find out. Dad's study was in the attic, and there was a window in the roof that would be possible to climb through.

I collected a knife from the kitchen and a rope from the garden shed. I ran through the sleeping house and up the stairs to Dad's study. I tied one end of the rope around my waist, and the other end to a leg of Dad's big, heavy old desk, which was under the window. Then I climbed out.

My trainers gripped the tiles quite well as I crept on to the roof. At first, I couldn't make out what the bundle was. I was on the wrong side of the chimney, so I couldn't see, but I didn't want to have to cling to it to work my way round it, in case I came face to face with... Goliath himself.

So, facing the slope of the roof, and leaning in towards it in a crouching position, I edged my

way along it not far above the gutter, my rope trailing behind me.

Then I saw Nick. He appeared to be clinging to the chimney stack for dear life. "Nick!" I called, but he didn't answer.

Cautiously, I crept closer. Then I could make out that Nick was gagged; he was making muffled noises but no real sound was coming out of his mouth. The gag looked like tape, or something, tied around his face. The same kind of tape tied him to the chimney stack.

As I crawled closer, Nick started shaking his head violently, and his eyes were bulging and scared. He kept nodding up at the chimney. I reached out and tried to pull away the tape that covered his mouth. It was disgusting and sticky, as though it had been soaked in treacle. He spat out bits of it.

"*Run!*" he hissed at me urgently. "The spider is in the chimney."

"I can't leave you here," I protested, hacking at

the tape that tied him to the brickwork with the kitchen knife. It dawned on me then that the tape was a spider's web, but it was like wire and almost impossible to cut.

As I pulled and tugged and sliced I caught something out of the corner of my eye, emerging from the top of the chimney. It was a spider's leg. A monstrous black spider leg with long brown hairs as sharp as the knife I was holding, and as thick as my wrist. It emerged slowly, a little at a time, testing the air, until it was longer than I am tall. It was followed by a second leg.

Delicately, the two legs touched the sides of the chimney and seemed to test their grip. They began to bend and strain as if levering something up behind them.

"Please run!" begged Nick. "You have to get away!" Before I could argue, he had pushed me with his free foot, and sent me sliding into the gutter, which began to pull away from the edge of the roof with my weight.

The gutter began bowing lower and lower beneath my feet and I heard a couple of brackets pull out of the wall. Suddenly, I was swinging from the end of my rope, over the side of the house.

"RU-U-U-UN!" screamed Nick. "He's after you!"

In a frantic moment, I imagined I could draw the spider away from Nick. I tried to undo the knot that bound me to the rope, but it was too tight from the tension caused by my weight. I hacked and hacked at the rope above it.

"The spider is coming!" shouted Nick. "Be quick! Be quick!"

"Dad!" I yelled. "Mum! Help!" I was hacking at the rope with my knife as hard as I could. I screamed and screamed for them, but Nick's sleeping mixture had made them sleep too soundly. I wanted to free myself and go and shake them awake, but if Goliath followed me to their bedroom, they might not wake up in time to defend themselves. I had to get Goliath away from the house.

"Go! Go!" cried Nick at the top of his lungs.

At last, I crashed to the ground, dropping the knife. I heard a thudding on the roof behind me. I had to get away! I took off as fast as my legs could carry me.

As I ran, I could still hear Nick screaming after me to run faster. I glanced over my shoulder and saw Goliath's dark shape looming behind me – the sleeping potion had made him clumsy.

I ran and ran until I couldn't hear Nick's voice any longer, and I finally reached the beach where I had found Dad's paperweight. I could hear the sound of crunching stones behind me. My heart was banging so hard I thought it would make a hole in my chest.

Frantically, I looked around for a way to escape. Then I saw it: a little rowing boat pulled up on the beach. I raced towards it, gathering all my strength to drag it across the stones and into the water. I pushed it out against the waves as far as I could – the water on my legs was freezing – then I threw myself over the side into the bottom.

The boat seemed to skid and slide on the surface of the water, as the currents took hold of it. For a moment I lay there. I wanted to look and see if the spider was on the beach, but I was too scared. So I lay for a few more seconds, my head buried in my arms, waiting for the current to carry me further out to sea. Had I been able to push the boat out far enough to be carried from the beach? I couldn't lie here for ever. Soon, I was going to have to take a look.

Slowly, I lifted my head. The boat was rising and falling heavily, so I knew I must be a little way from the shore. I peered over the edge of the boat and froze – there was no spider on the beach at all!

What if it had gone back for Nick? Even worse, what if the sound of crunching stones behind me had only been my imagination, and it had never followed me at all? Quickly, I fished around amongst the ropes and fishing tackle in the water swilling in the bottom of the boat to find oars, or anything that I could use to row me back to shore.

I kicked against something hard, like a bump or lump, and dislodged it. It was an odd-looking, slightly familiar object. Right now, I couldn't think what it was, and I didn't care, but I put it in my pocket anyway.

I had to hurry now as the boat seemed suddenly to be taking on more water. There were no oars in it, but as I glanced up, I saw what looked like oars slotted, somehow, into the sides of the boat, sticking upwards. My hair was wet and in my eyes, and in a panic, I was rushing; I just had to get home. I grabbed at an oar.

As I did so, I realised there were seven other oars placed evenly around the edge of the boat, it was then I knew that if I looked up, I would see Goliath standing over me like a gigantic black hand! If I looked, I would be frozen with fear. The oar beneath my fingers was not an oar at all…

I tore my hand away, crawled to the gap

between two of the legs and threw myself over the side. The water was grey and icy, it was still early in the morning and there was no sun. The coldness of the water knocked the breath out of me for a moment, but then I was swimming, swimming as if my life depended on it, which it did. I didn't dare look back. This was what I thought it must feel like to be chased by a shark.

I knew I had to swim hard, because of the undertow being so strong. Even though it felt as if I wasn't getting anywhere, I carried on, doggedly pulling my arms through the water, dragging myself towards the beach. I couldn't give in, or I'd be gone.

* * * *

At last I was on the beach, gasping for breath. I collapsed in a shivering, wet heap on the stones and looked back to see where the boat was. Maybe the spider was rowing back? Maybe he could swim? I remembered Nick playing with little spiders. The ones which could walk on water because their feet didn't break the skin on the surface.

I spotted the boat easily. It was definitely sinking. As I strained my eyes to see the spider, the boat was overturned by a wave – and I could see nothing inside it.

Then I waited, and waited. I had to make sure the 'thing' wasn't going to crawl out of the water again. I sat there for what seemed like ages, but the spider never reappeared.

****

I was woken by Mum putting a blanket around me. I had fallen asleep from exhaustion. The pebbles were digging into my sides and I was numb with cold. Dad scooped me up in his arms and carried me off the beach. And there was Nick, trailing after us. He'd guessed where I would run to, and had brought Mum and Dad with him to find me.

I had no idea what we were going to tell them as I walked the last bit home, clutching the blanket around my shoulders.

"Want to tell us why you were playing a game where you tied your brother to the chimney?" asked Mum, with a furious expression on her face. "I can't believe the noise didn't wake us!"

Even Dad was tight-lipped with fury, although he kept an arm around me as if he thought I might slip away back into the sea.

I glanced at Nick, who shrugged. I wondered if the whole thing was a dream from the beginning.

"Nick and I were playing a stupid dare game, where I bet him he wouldn't climb on to the roof — and it ended up with me tying him to the chimney," I began lamely. "Then I decided to scare him by leaving him there for a bit, and went for a swim. But I got caught in the undertow and nearly didn't make it..." My voice trailed off.

Dad and Mum looked at each other. I knew they didn't believe me. "I think we're going to have to lay down some new ground rules when we get home," Mum told me grimly.

* * * *

Mum sent me upstairs to get into some dry clothes and Nick came running after me.

"What happened?" he asked excitedly. "Where is Goliath?"

I told him how I'd pushed the boat out, only to find the spider had jumped aboard, then how I'd had to swim for it. Suddenly, I remembered the thing in my pocket.

"Here," I told him, "you have this, I found it in the bottom of the boat."

Nick took it, curious. He frowned, looking puzzled, then he began to laugh. "It's the rubber bung from the bottom of the boat!" he exclaimed. "It's there to block up the hole."

"Hole?" I asked. He wasn't making any sense.

"Those little rowing boats have holes in the bottom so they can drain out the sea water that splashes in, when they get back to shore," he told me. "When you pulled this out, you sank the boat!"

Now I realised what the object reminded me of — a bath plug.

I heard Dad in the hallway downstairs. "I can't get the living room fire to light," he called to Mum. "The chimney seems to be blocked. I just wanted to get Sarah warmed up in front of it."

"We should have had the chimney swept!" I heard Mum reply.

"It's probably something Goliath left behind," I muttered to Nick. A strange expression crossed his face for an instant as an unpleasant thought occurred to him.

"We just assumed Goliath was a male spider," he said slowly. "But what if he wasn't? What if 'he' was a 'she' and 'she' made a nest?"

I could feel all the colour drain from my face. "Wait while I change into something dry," I instructed him. It only took me seconds.

Downstairs again, we pulled the fireguard away from the fireplace in the living room and swept aside the sticks and paper Dad had been using to get a fire going. We peered up the chimney with a torch, but there was a bend in it, and it wasn't possible to see anything.

Nick followed me up to Dad's study. Fortunately, Dad had left for work now, and Mum was downstairs getting breakfast ready.

We clambered out on to the roof. The sense of urgency made me feel almost unafraid as we peered down the chimney. It had been big enough for the spider to get in and out of, and now I could understand why the rain used to run down inside and splash in the grate sometimes.

"I still can't see anything," complained Nick. "But it doesn't mean to say there's nothing there."

"So what do we do?" I asked him.

"We drop something down there to push it out," he replied.

"And what if there IS something there, and they've all hatched, and we scatter them all over the place?" I asked uneasily. Nick didn't reply.

He clambered back into the study, and re-emerged with a box of matches from Dad's desk drawer, and a few sheets of paper. He screwed the sheets of paper into long twists, then lit them, one by one, and dropped them down the chimney.

Then we scrambled back inside, and ran down to the living room. Nothing happened for a while.

Soon, there was this scuffling and scraping sound. It got louder and louder as it came down the chimney. My heart was in my mouth as I realised it had almost reached the fireplace. Quickly, Nick pulled the bits of wood and paper Dad had been using, into a pile again, and threw a lighted match onto it.

The smell from the chimney was terrible; like burning wool. There were strange sounds like tiny voices calling from a long way off, and the room was filling with smoke.

Just as Mum put her head round the door to see what we were up to, a cloud of soot descended from the chimney. In it, landing with a sickening squashy sound into the beginnings of our small fire, was a smouldering spider egg-sack, like a gigantic cotton-wool ball full of little black shapes that sparked every time one caught alight.

"Oh no," sighed Mum, "it must be an old bird's nest!"

Nick and I watched the ball curl and twist in its own heat, as the singed and burning parts worked their way through the many hundreds of fuzzy black spots that were baby spiders hatching. I was sure they would have grown as fast as their mother had.

Just as the cotton wool seemed to have been crisped and blackened until there was nothing much left except a fragile tissue of black ash, a small spider scuttled out of the fireplace and across the floor. Even as it ran, it appeared to be getting larger.

Nick jumped to his feet and was about to stamp on it. But Mum grabbed him. "If you want to live and thrive," she told him firmly, "let a spider run alive. It's an old proverb you should listen to."

"Not THIS time!" cried Nick leaping onto the scuttling creature, and squashing it flat.

****

For his birthday, Dad got the stone paperweight from me, and a flat spider set in perspex from Nick. It looked like a black pressed flower with eight thin petals.

As for the rabbits, they grew huge. I panicked a bit because they seemed to grow so fast, and I was worried about Nick. If one of the less treated of his tomatoes affected the bunnies so badly, how would HE be affected?

One day, I called him into my room to have a look. "I hope the spider was only affected because he ate the concentrated mixture," I said. "But look at the size of the rabbits! What are we going to do if you grow, too?"

Nick grinned. "It's quite all right," he assured me, "the spider really WAS only affected because of the concentrated mixture in the dead plant. These rabbits are just fine, and I don't seem to have grown any taller, do I?"

No, Nick didn't SEEM to be any taller. But the rabbits really WERE getting bigger.

"They are giant rabbits," Nick laughed. "They are going to get HUGE all on their own."

As Nick walked out, I had to rub my eyes; the trousers he was wearing no longer quite covered his ankles...

Feathers

Julie was lying on her bed reading, when she heard her parents arguing about something. Curious, she left her book on the bed, and crept to the top of the stairs where she could hear better.

"My mother cannot come and live with us, and that's that!" Mrs Jackson insisted.

"But she's only an old woman, and now your grandmother's dead, she's all on her own," Mr Jackson replied. "We have that huge back room upstairs. We only keep junk in it. We can easily move all that into the attic."

"Is someone dead?" asked Julie, finding them in the kitchen. "I couldn't help overhearing."

"Your great-grandmother, my grandmother, died two weeks ago," replied her mother shortly.

"So your mother is coming to live with us?" cried Julie excitedly. "I'd love to meet my only remaining grandmother! Sally's grandmother bought her a pony last year. I always thought it was really bad luck that mine lived in another country."

"Your grandmother isn't that kind of person," said Julie's mother in a warning tone.

★★★★

That afternoon, Julie found her mother half-heartedly packing some of the junk in the spare room into a cardboard box.

"What does Granny look like? Do you have a photograph?" Julie asked. Her mother looked blank for a minute.

"She looks a bit like me, but twenty-two years

older," she replied. "And no, I've never kept a photograph of her." Out of a pile of papers that Mrs Jackson threw into the box, there floated a long, brown bird's feather.

Julie picked it up. "Wow, look at this!" she cried, "can I keep it?"

Her mother snatched it from her with surprising speed, and threw it in the box.

"It's only an old bird's feather," she said, sounding irritated.

****

That afternoon, Julie decided to take another look at the feather.

Up in the spare room, she rummaged through the box – through her father's old business accounts, some old school exercise books and some letters written to her parents.

Most of the letters were really boring, like the one from a friend called Edith talking about the vet operating on her dog, or a distant cousin sending her a horrible, once-a-year, computer-printout Christmas letter, the one that told everyone everything, even how they'd unblocked their own drains!

But then she found a couple of letters written in a strange, shaky hand and forgot all about the feather. The address on the backs of the envelopes said they were from someone called Leonie, in Papua New Guinea, but the letters inside were signed "Mother". Quickly, Julie read through them.

They were letters from Julie's grandmother, one was letting Julie's mother know how Great-gran was, and talked about a cat, or something, called Alfred. But the other letter asked if Julie's mother had received the photographs safely.

Julie rummaged through the box again. This time she found another envelope, with writing on it like the other two, tucked down the side of the box.

Unfolding the letter, she saw three

photographs. One was of an apple tree flowering in someone's garden, its boughs of pink blossom weighing the young tree down. Another showed the front of a single- storey house with a very neat front lawn and a cactus growing thin and tall, to one side of the doorway. The last photograph was of two women standing side-by-side outside the same house.

The younger of the two women was extremely pretty, and looked not much older than Julie's mother did now. She must have injured herself somehow, because she was wearing a bandage that covered one of her bare arms from the wrist to the elbow. The other woman appeared to be much older, but it was quite hard to tell. Even in the brilliant sunshine captured by the camera, the second woman was wrapped bulkily in black trousers, black pullovers and a black coat. There was a black scarf wrapped tightly round her neck, a flat brimmed, floppy black hat on her head, and she wore dark glasses.

Julie read the letter; the young woman was her grandmother, and the bundled-up woman was her great-grandmother who had just died.

Julie replaced the letters, but she hid the photo of the two women in her bedroom. Her mother had obviously forgotten about it, so she wouldn't miss it.

Two days later, a taxi pulled up outside the door, and out of it got a strange-looking woman. Julie was staring out of her bedroom window in disbelief, it was the OLDER woman in the photograph. She ran and got the photo out, just to make sure. Yes, the woman was identical, right down to the floppy black hat and the sunglasses.

"Mum!" she shouted, "Great-granny is here!" Mrs Jackson hurriedly joined her at the window.

"That's not Great-granny, your great-granny died, remember? That's your grandmother."

"But..." protested Julie.

"But what?" asked her mother. Julie bit her lip and decided not to say anything.

****

She reached the front door just as her mother was telling her grandmother she definitely could not stay.

"But I have come to stay with my only daughter," the old woman replied from the muffle of her scarf. "Just like my mother came to live with me. You know we always look after each other. How can you turn me away when I have travelled so far?"

"Come on in, Leonie!" Mr Jackson called from the hallway. "I think you just took us by surprise, we weren't expecting you yet."

The old lady, covered in black from head to toe and wearing gloves, pushed past Julie and Mrs Jackson. Mr Jackson went to shake her hand, and Julie stuck out her hand to be shaken, too. Gran began taking her gloves off.

"Don't do that!" cried Mrs Jackson. Everyone stared at her. "You're not staying! So there's no point in taking your gloves off."

"Mum," said Julie, "the taxi driver left a whole pile of luggage by the front door. It looks like Granny has come to stay for good." There was a long, awkward silence while they all stood around in the hall looking silly.

"Well," said Mr Jackson at last, "you can stay for a while. The spare room is nearly cleaned out, it won't take long to finish, will it Julie?"

Julie shook her head and went up to pack the last bits and pieces into the box so it could be put in the attic.

Two minutes later, Julie's mother appeared in the doorway. "I need to talk to you, darling," she whispered, sitting by Julie on the spare bed. "It's about your grandmother."

"What about her?" asked Julie.

"Your grandmother has a rare skin condition," Mrs Jackson explained, "and it's highly, highly contagious. While she's here, it is terribly, terribly important that you don't touch her. Really she should go to a nursing home or something, where they can look after her."

"Does Daddy know?" asked Julie.

"I've just told him," her mother replied.

****

On the phone to her friend Sally, Julie tried to describe her grandmother, but Sally didn't believe her.

"She CAN'T be cold, wrapped up in all those clothes, it's the middle of summer!" Sally argued.

"Maybe it's because of her skin condition," suggested Julie, "or because she's used to living in a hot country — but she certainly doesn't need her sunglasses indoors."

****

When Gran appeared at the dinner table, she was still wearing her sunglasses.

"Granny, why have you got those on?" asked Julie. "They must make it very hard to see properly."

Now the scarf-wrapped neck turned the huge, hatted head towards Julie. Nothing was visible through the dark glass of the spectacles.

"My eyes are sensitive to light," said the old woman. Her voice sounded like a brick being dragged along concrete on the end of a piece of string. Julie supposed her light-sensitive eyes might be a result of her skin condition.

In truth, Julie was dying to have a look at the disease her mother had mentioned, but her Gran was so well wrapped up, not a bit of flesh showed anywhere, except for a little bit on her face, and that just looked as though it was very, very old and wrinkly.

Granny had an amazing appetite for an old lady. She ate everything, picking each bit of food up with her gloved fingers and cramming it into her mouth. She had atrocious table manners, but nobody commented.

Marmaduke, Julie's ginger cat, found it was profitable to sit beneath the table by Granny. He ate all the food that fell from the old woman's fingers, until Granny noticed and kicked him out of the way.

Julie heard the 'whuuuuuf' of Marmaduke's breath as it was knocked out of him. "Don't do that!" she cried. But Granny ignored her and carried on eating.

Marmaduke picked himself up and limped into the hallway.

Sally came round for an hour afterwards, wanting to have a look at Julie's granny, but the old woman had gone back to her room.

"I'll show you what she looks like," grinned Julie, taking Sally to her bedroom where she had hidden the photograph.

Sally studied the picture of the two women. "Does she look anything like she did when she was younger?" she asked.

Julie shook her head. "Not at all, in fact, she looks so like Great-gran, it's hard to tell them apart. Even the clothes look the same."

"Maybe your gran died, not her mother," suggested Sally. "Maybe your great-gran is immortal, and is pretending to be your gran, so she doesn't look suspicious."

Julie just laughed.

****

It was in the early hours of the morning, that Julie heard noises from the kitchen. She crept downstairs to see who it was, only to find her grandmother, still dressed in all her clothes and wearing her dark glasses, eating raw liver out of the fridge. Blood was running down her chin as she sucked each slimy piece into her mouth. She wasn't wearing her gloves, and in the light from the fridge, her long nails were visible, and her arthritic, swollen, distorted knuckles.

The backs of her hands looked as if they were made of old, cracked leather. She didn't notice Julie, so Julie quietly crept away again.

In the morning, it was Julie's mother who looked as though she had been up all night. Julie noticed her father's worried expression and felt a sense of unease pass over her.

Mrs Jackson prepared a breakfast tray to take to Gran's room. "I'll take that, Mum," offered Julie, but her mother just shook her head.

"Well, I don't know if she'll be hungry anyway," Julie said. "I saw her last night, eating raw meat out of the fridge. I think it was liver or something, so we won't have any left if you wanted it for supper tonight."

Mrs Jackson opened the fridge to check, and pulled out the bloody wrapper of what had, indeed, been liver. She took the breakfast tray in anyway, with bacon, eggs and toast. Julie noticed she was wearing rubber gloves that covered her wrists and hands, and a long-sleeved top.

Before Julie had even left for school, Granny let out a long, hoarse cry, for Mrs Jackson to come and collect her empty tray.

****

"The old woman has only been with us two weeks," complained Julie, "and it's as if she's been here for months. And she's never leaving. Mum was right, she's a miserable old woman and Mum looks really tired all the time. What's really weird, is the way she watches me. And Mum watches her watching me."

****

That evening Julie was sent to call her grandmother for dinner, but, her mother instructed, she was not to go into the room.

Julie stood outside the door. "Gran," she called softly, "Gran?" but there was no answer.

"Gran?" she called, a little louder this time. Still no answer.

"GRAN!" But STILL no reply. Slowly, Julie turned the door handle.

"WHAT DO YOU THINK YOU ARE DOING!" demanded her mother, appearing suddenly behind her. "I told you not to go into the room under any circumstances."

"But she might be ill, or something," protested Julie, "because she's not answering."

Mrs Jackson flung the door open. Inside, the curtains were drawn and the room was in almost total blackness.

Granny was a bulk of bedclothes on the bed. "Dinner is ready!" bellowed Mrs Jackson.

"I think I want to stay here," said a hoarse, wheedling voice from the bed. "Why don't you send Julie in with a tray?"

"I shall do nothing of the sort," replied Julie's mother. "I will bring it myself."

"I don't mind Mum, really," Julie insisted. But her mother wouldn't hear of it.

As she closed the door, Mrs Jackson moved the key from the inside of the room, to the outside, and locked it, dropping the key into her trouser pocket.

"If she can't behave, she will have to stay in her room," said Mrs Jackson firmly.

When she took the supper tray to her mother, Mrs Jackson wore rubber gloves again.

While she was gone, Julie found the long, brown feather in Marmaduke's bed. It was slightly chewed. Julie couldn't work out how he had managed to dig the feather out from the box which was now in the attic. She took it to school with her the next morning.

****

During lunch, Julie told Sally all about her mother keeping her grandmother in a locked room.

"I wish I knew what was really happening," she complained. "Mum and Dad don't tell me anything."

The two girls asked the biology teacher about the feather. Old Mr Wilson stared at it for a long time.

"Where did you say you found it?" he asked.

"In the cat's basket in the kitchen," Julie replied. "But it came from a box in the attic."

"Well, it didn't come from any bird around here," he told her. "It is very much like one of the larger raptor-type birds. The sort you find in Africa."

"What's a raptor?" asked Sally.

"A large meat-eating bird," said Mr Wilson. "Like I said, there's nothing like that around here."

****

When Julie got home, she found the box from the spare room just inside the door to the attic. She opened it up and put the feather in. But there, sticking out of one corner, was the first feather. There were two of them now. So where did the second one come from?

****

In the morning, Marmaduke had gone – Julie

couldn't find him anywhere. All that was left was a clump of bloody hair in the corner of his basket, which she showed to her mother.

Mrs Jackson studied it for a bit, though her expression gave nothing away. "Oh, dear," she said vaguely, "it looks as though Marmaduke has been in a fight." She threw the clump of fur in the bin.

★★★★

That evening, Marmaduke still hadn't come home. Julie's father suggested he might be off somewhere licking his wounds. After supper, while it was still light, Sally came to help Julie stick up little posters in the street, asking if anyone had seen a ginger cat.

★★★★

It took Julie a while to get to sleep that night, and no sooner was she asleep, than she was woken sharply by a hand around her wrist, dragging her

out of bed. It held her in a vice-like grip and shook her. She let out a loud wail, then another hand clamped around her mouth.

Just for a moment, the hand on her mouth released her, and she smelt the foul, bitter odour of Granny's breath directly on her face. She spluttered and fought to get away, but the hand that kept her suspended, half-sitting, half-standing on the bed, was as strong as iron.

"Too late, little one," hissed Granny, pushing her down again.

Julie lunged for her bedside light and switched it on. There, standing over her, all wrapped up in her black clothes and still wearing her black glasses, was the old woman. She appeared much taller tonight, drawn up as she was, to her full height.

"What are you doing in my room!" Julie demanded weakly.

"Just coming to visit," answered the old crone, folding her bare hands together. Now visible, they looked like tree bark, all gnarled, Julie supposed, by the skin disease.

"Oh no!" Julie cried, suddenly remembering. "Your disease is contagious!"

The old woman laughed out loud. "Is that what your mother told you? Ha!"

"Well, isn't it?" demanded Julie, staring at her wrist, waiting for the first sign of a rash, or something.

The noise had brought Julie's parents running. Her father grabbed the old woman and literally dragged her out of the room. Julie's mother hurried to the bed and swept Julie into her arms, hugging her so tightly she almost couldn't breathe.

"Tell me what she did!" she urged Julie. "I need to know everything."

"Well, if her skin thing's contagious," Julie replied, "you probably shouldn't be touching me." She explained how Gran had hauled her out of bed.

Slowly, Mrs Jackson let go of her daughter and Julie's heart sank at the expression on her mother's face.

"It'll probably be fine," said Mrs Jackson unconvincingly. "I'm just over-cautious when it comes to anything that might make you sick. We'll keep a close eye on you, but it's probably nothing at all to worry about."

****

So Julie didn't worry. Much. In the morning she saw that Gran's door had been forced open from the inside. The door frame was splintered and torn. Now there was a huge padlock on it to keep it closed.

****

As the days went by, Julie almost forgot about what had happened. Her skin looked fine, so she wasn't worried. From time to time, she remembered Marmaduke and went out looking for him, but without success. Mrs Jackson said it was probably because he'd been frightened by whatever he'd had a fight with, and wandered off.

★★★★

Then one day, Sally and Julie were in the school changing rooms getting ready for basketball, when Sally noticed what looked like a bruise on Julie's arm.

"It's probably where Granny grabbed me," Julie explained. "It can take a while for bruises to show, you know."

"It doesn't take over a week, though," Sally pointed out.

Julie showed her mother when she got home, and Mrs Jackson agreed that it probably was a bruise, and bandaged it.

"Bruises don't need bandages!" protested Julie. Her mother insisted that this one did.

And when it got bigger, Mrs Jackson put a bigger bandage on it, and some skin cream.

Sally said it reminded her of the bandage Julie's grandmother had on her arm in the old photograph.

"Coincidence," muttered Julie.

Julie's mother insisted she mustn't take the bandage off. "Your grandmother really gave you a good bruising," she told her. "The cream I put on your arm will help draw it out."

"Why did Granny do what she did?" asked Julie.

"Because she's nasty," was the short reply, "and she shouldn't be here."

* * * *

Julie found she wasn't sleeping well at night; she was really cold and it kept her awake — though the weather was wonderfully warm.

When she fell asleep in her maths lesson for the second time, she was sent to the headmaster for a warning. "Next time," he informed her, "it'll be a detention."

When she got home, she decided it was high time she had a look at her bruise to see if it was getting better.

She managed to untie the knot that held the bandage, and slowly unwound it, peering closely at her skin as she did so.

The first centimetre or so, looked perfectly all right. Then, as more appeared, the skin colour changed dramatically. It was a muddy, soupy, browny yellow. Julie smiled to herself, she knew that old bruises always went kind of yellowy and blotchy around the edges as they were getting better...

****

So when Sally wanted to have another look a couple of days later, Julie was almost sure the bruise would be pretty well gone altogether. She undid the knot again, and unwound the bandage.

"Well?" she asked Sally. "Do you think it's getting better?"

Sally was as pale as a ghost. She put her hand over her mouth. "*Ugh*," she said, "it looks as though it's gone bad, or something."

"Bruises don't go bad," snapped Julie, taking a closer look at her half-unbandaged arm. She nearly fell off her chair. The bruise had got MUCH worse! Quickly, she covered it up again.

"I think I need to go to the doctor!" she told her mother when she got home. Mrs Jackson wiped an eye, shaking her head.

"It wouldn't do any good, darling," she told Julie gently.

"You mean I have Granny's skin problem, DON'T you!" demanded Julie.

Her mother nodded.

"But there MUST be a cure!" wailed Julie. "Or am I going to end up all covered up like she is?"

"I'm going to see what can be done," her mother said gently, "but you have to trust me, and it will take time."

"Granny infected me on purpose!" cried Julie. "WHY?"

"One of the symptoms of the illness is that the personality changes," her mother explained. "It turns a perfectly nice person into a pretty horrible one."

"So I'm going to become horrible?" asked Julie. Her mother shrugged helplessly.

That night Julie lay in bed, thinking and thinking. She was going to change. What was she really going to look like? The unknown is always much worse than the known, isn't it? If she knew what was going to happen to her, maybe it would help.

She waited until her parents had been in bed for a least an hour, then she crept downstairs to the kitchen, where, high on a hook, hung the key to the padlock on the spare-room door.

Upstairs, she quietly unlocked the padlock, and pushed the door open.

Inside, the room was in total darkness, the

curtains were drawn and the windows were closed. It was the smell that hit Julie first. She gagged, and put her hand over her nose and mouth. The stench was foul.

For one horrible moment, she imagined her grandmother had been dead for a while.

Then there was a slight movement from the bed. Ever so slight, but enough to make her think there was something alive in the room.

"Granny?" hissed Julie, but the old woman didn't answer. Trying desperately to breathe through the smell, Julie stepped further into the room, squinting into the darkness. She tried the light switch but the bulb was out. *"Granny,"* Julie whispered again. Still no reply. Now she was worried her parents might wake up.

Fumbling for a handhold, she stumbled into something. Looking down, she could make out that it was a bucket. A bucket filled with a sticky, sloppy stuff. The smell intensified for a moment, it seemed to be coming from the bucket. Feeling sicker by the minute, Julie realised her mother must have left it in here for her grandmother to use as a toilet. How else was the old woman to go to the loo if she was padlocked in her bedroom?

Julie felt strangely giddy at the thought of her parents imprisoning her grandmother. She'd seen this sort of thing on the news on TV but it happened to other people, it never happened to you. Determined now, Julie made her way to the window and pulled the curtains back. Moonlight streamed into the room.

Suddenly, there was an unholy screech from the bed, and Granny sat up, pulling the covers over her head. "Too bright! Too bright!" she cried in a strange, hoarse voice.

Julie shut the curtains half-way. "*Granny*, I need to talk to you," she whispered urgently, her knees weak and her hands sweating a cold sweat.

The old woman remained huddled, but peered over the top of the mound of blankets. She must have been freezing, because she was still in her clothes and her hat. She smelt pretty awful, but it was a different kind of smell from the stuff in the bucket. More of a stale smell, as if she hadn't had a bath for weeks — which of course she probably hadn't, since Julie had never seen her use the bathroom.

"I want to know," began Julie unsteadily, "why you gave me your rash on purpose."

"I didn't give you a rash," said the old woman, a smile in her voice. Julie shivered, more with cold than fear; the cold was REALLY getting to her now, even with a pullover over her nightie.

"I didn't give you a rash at all!" laughed Granny. "I gave you Alfred!"

"*What*? Who's Alfred?" demanded Julie, thinking the old woman must be quite demented.

"Alfred lives here, with us," Granny replied.

"Stop that right now!" barked Julie's mother from the doorway. Both parents stood there, Mr Jackson rubbing his eyes wearily. Mrs Jackson told him to check on her mother, while she took Julie back to bed. The old woman raised a fist and shook it. A long chain rattled, and to her horror, Julie saw that Granny was chained to the iron bedstead.

****

When they were alone, Julie's mother took her hand. "Alfred," she began, "has been with the women of this family for centuries. He's a spirit. He, well… sort of possesses us."

"I don't want to be possessed!" wailed Julie, wondering if Alfred was here now.

"He lived inside your great-grandmother until her death, then he moved into your granny. If he had nowhere to go, he would die, but he never dies because we always have more children. Maybe we shouldn't, but each of us hopes we'll have a boy. He can only inhabit the girls in the family, it's something to do with our blood type.

"Your grandmother passed the beginning of

him on to you, when she came to your room. She must have breathed on you when she woke you up. It takes touch and breath together to transfer Alfred."

"She did," said Julie miserably. "But why didn't he move into you?"

"Because I would never touch my mother or allow her to breathe on me. I never got close," Mrs Jackson replied. "And I always wore a scarf around my face when I was in the bedroom with Mother."

"But won't you be in trouble now you've touched me?" asked Julie.

Her mother shook her head. "Alfred has to be concentrated in just one person before he can move on to another. He could only move to me, if he was all in you, or if he moved himself completely back to Granny. Oh dear, who would have thought an old lady could break the door open?"

"So Alfred could move back to *Granny*?" Julie said hopefully. Mrs Jackson replied that it was unlikely when he had the choice between a young girl and an old lady.

"Can't we kill him?" asked Julie.

Mrs Jackson told her how the family had tried for years, but since Alfred was a spirit, it was pretty impossible. They had even tried exorcism with a priest on at least two occasions.

"So what will happen to me now?" Julie demanded fearfully. Her mother took the bandage off her daughter's arm. Underneath, was a foul and puckered brown skin, layered with spiky feathers.

"You mean I'll have *feathers*?!" Julie screeched. She stared at them closely. Gingerly, she felt the little spiky hair follicles around the larger feathers — it was as if they were about to bloom.

She glanced down at her legs beneath her nightdress. Her right leg was crawling with the same rash that looked like a bruise and her left leg was showing pink patches.

All night, after her mother had left her, Julie tossed and turned, her mind whirring. There was always a solution to a problem, she thought, always. It's just that sometimes it wasn't easy to find. Sometimes it wasn't obvious...

****

Mrs Jackson let Sally come and visit while she went shopping, having sworn her to secrecy. Sally sat in Julie's bedroom, staring at her friend's arms and legs. The small feathers were quite formed and visible now, and the larger ones were getting even bigger.

"If I hadn't seen it with my own eyes," Sally said, "I simply wouldn't have believed it. Even your eyes look different; sort of hooded."

"I tried shaving the feathers off with Dad's razor, but they just bleed," said Julie miserably. Just then, her father put his head round the door. Julie tried to cover her arms and legs but she wasn't quick enough.

"Your mother always warned me about this, but I never really believed her," he said, shocked, coming over to give Julie a hug. "We're going to try and find a solution to this, one way or another," he added grimly.

"Maybe there's something in the letter that came with the photo which might help?" asked Sally. Julie had forgotten all about the letter, and there were the other letters, too.

Julie's father brought the box down from the attic. Together, the three of them began searching the letters for clues.

Julie thought she could remember the name "Alfred" from one of them. Sure enough, Granny had written to Julie's mother when Julie was born, telling her that if she hadn't had any children, Alfred would have been brought to a halt.

"He's like a cat, who passes from lap to lap as each of us dies, always moving on just before it's too late. If he had nowhere to move on to, then he would surely end," Julie read from the letter.

"And if any one of us were to remain separated from the family, he would certainly die. But when possessed we become selfish and foul — we *want* to move Alfred on, and the sooner the better. We become Alfred's slaves and cannot save our loved ones."

"If Alfred thought me and Mum were going to die," Julie said, thinking out loud, "then he might just move back to Granny, which is where he should be. At least we could put him off for a bit longer."

"How are we supposed to do that?" asked Sally.

"Pretend you're going to hit me with something heavy," suggested Julie. Sally and Mr Jackson looked at her as though she'd gone mad.

"Do it!" cried Julie in exasperation. "Like you say, we haven't got a lot to lose. You only have to pretend, just make it look good."

"But what if the 'Alfred' can hear?" asked Sally, half joking. But Julie took her seriously.

"I'm guessing that he hasn't all moved in yet, since I still feel like me," she smiled.

Mr Jackson watched, curious, as Sally picked up a small brass figure from a table, and pretended she was going to hit Julie with it. It was amazing, the feathery rash that was about to receive the blow, faded almost instantly, and moved slightly to one side.

"It looks as if Sally would have to hit you all over," said Mr Jackson. "It's weird, it's almost as if the feathers can SEE. It's as if they just moved out of the way."

"You need to make Alfred think you're really going to die, but slowly enough for him to leave and move back to your gran," said Sally, thoughtfully. "What else do we know about him?"

"He doesn't like the cold," Mr Jackson reminded them. "Remember how much your grandmother has to wrap up in all those clothes? And Julie, you're freezing all the time now."

Julie looked at him and grinned, her face lit up.

"I think I've got it!" she cried. Sally and Mr Jackson followed Julie to the utility room where they kept the big chest freezer. Before anyone could ask why, she had opened the freezer and was pulling out frozen pizzas and quiches — she left the frozen meat and bags of vegetables, which she stacked around the sides so there was a dip in the middle.

Then she climbed in and lay down.

"That's stupid!" cried Sally, "you'll freeze to death!"

"That's what she wants Alfred to think," said Mr Jackson quietly.

Shivering like mad, her teeth chattering, and getting unbearably cold, Julie lay quite still. Minute by minute, the rash and the little feather-ends, appeared to subside.

"That's remarkable," her father gasped, watching a little red patch turn pink, then white.

"You'll have to stop Mum from going anywhere near Granny when she comes home," said Julie, "or Alfred will try to infect her too, when he's back in Granny."

Soon, they heard Mrs Jackson opening the front door. Sally ran to tell her not to go near Granny, and tried to explain what Julie was doing.

Mrs Jackson thought the whole idea was preposterous. She stormed into the utility room and ordered Julie to get out of the freezer before she did herself some serious damage.

"But look at her!" Mr Jackson cried.

Mrs Jackson had another look at her daughter and saw that she was almost completely free of feathers.

"It's justtttt so-oo-oo-oo-oo-ooo cold!" she shivered. As she spoke, there was an ear-splitting howl from Gran's room.

Mrs Jackson was about to run and look, but Mr Jackson pushed her back and ordered her to stay away. "That's what she wants!" he cried. He ran to look himself, kicking the door in as he had no time to get the padlock key.

In front of him, taking up the whole double bed, was a gigantic bird with a beak like a pickaxe. Feathers were sprouting and wings were shaking. There were no fingers inside the gloves now. They lay ripped apart on the floor. The whole quivering mass was balancing on a pair of the most enormous claws that had pierced right through the bedclothes and into the mattress.

As soon as the bird-creature saw Julie's father, it let out the most harrowing screech and launched itself at him, dragging filthy, torn blankets and sheets after it and scattering tufts of ginger cat hair. The "Alfred" inside Granny… was a vulture.

Now, Granny's neck unwound its bald stem from the folds of the scarf she wore, and shot forwards in an attempt to propel the hooked beak into Mr Jackson's shoulder. The chain around its wing snapped, letting it free. Mr Jackson turned and ran.

He intended to escape out of the back door of the kitchen, but he saw the bird-thing had turned towards the utility room.

He leaped, grabbing it by the huge feathers of its shoulders, but they came away in his hands. Now the bird-thing had found Julie in the freezer. As she was free of feathers, it was going to have to infect her all over again. With another cry of fury, the bird-creature hauled her out of the freezer with its beak, and flung her to the floor. It was just about to breathe into Julie's face again, as it held her down with its talons, when Mrs Jackson flung herself at the bird, and it turned on her instead. In the nick of time, as it gripped Julie's mother in a huge claw, about to breathe into her face, Mr Jackson knocked it over.

The flailing bird toppled into the freezer and, as quick as a snake, Sally slammed the lid shut, and Mr Jackson sat on it.

"You look better," gasped Mr Jackson, staring hard at his daughter, as she picked herself off the floor. He wiped the sweat off his forehead with his shirt sleeves.

"That's why your grandmother got worse," observed Sally, handing her cardigan to Julie to put round her shivering shoulders.

Granny was now banging on the lid of the freezer from inside.

"What shall we do with her?" asked Mrs Jackson.

"We can't let her out yet," her husband replied. "She was trying to kill us. What if we tied the freezer door down, and took her to the police?"

"Daddy, they would never believe us!" cried Julie.

"They'd have to," Sally pointed out, "if you had a two-metre-tall vulture, frozen like a popsicle!"

No one wanted to move. No one wanted to let the horrible creature out again. As they sat there, the banging subsided.

"She's probably suffocated," muttered Sally hopefully.

They listened for what seemed like an age. "Let's take a look," Julie ventured at last.

Mr Jackson slid off the top of the freezer.

Gingerly, he lifted the lid a tiny bit. Nothing happened.

"But what if she's just pretending to be frozen?" whispered Sally.

Julie shuddered as Mr Jackson lifted the lid a bit more… then a bit more… Nothing.

Then it was open all the way.

There, lying in the freezer, its eyes open and staring vacantly, its beak ajar, was the bird-thing. Julie reached out to touch it, but Mr Jackson snatched her hand back.

"I don't trust your grandmother," he told her.

Mrs Jackson peered over his shoulder.

"If only," she said, "this really could be the end of it."

It seemed as though the vulture creature was indeed, dead. But then Julie saw something. "Look!" she cried. "Its chest feathers are moving!"

Everyone stepped back a bit.

They watched as the feathers rose slightly, as if the bird-thing was taking a deep breath. Suddenly, there was a small voice, almost like a child's: "Help! Let me out!"

Mrs Jackson listened intently. "Mother?" she whispered.

"Please, let me out!" cried the far-away voice

Mrs Jackson dived towards the heap of feathers in the freezer and began tearing at them as if she was unstuffing some gigantic pillow, until at last she had ripped a pathway through.

There, curled up inside the remains of the bird-thing, was the old woman, trying to cover herself with a few loose feathers.

Quickly, Mrs Jackson grabbed a towel from a pile of laundry on the floor, and threw it into the freezer, tucking it around the little figure inside.

"*Granny*?" Julie whispered in amazement.

Granny was helped out of the freezer.

The dainty old lady looked down at all the feathers. "What happened?" she asked shakily.

"You mean, you don't remember?" asked Julie.

Granny shook her head.

"I'm Julie," grinned Julie. "And you're my grandmother."

The old lady gave her granddaughter a tearful hug.

Sally left them to their weepy reunion. Granny, as it turned out, didn't remember anything since she'd first got her feathers, ages and ages ago.

****

It took two days to clear up the mess in the spare room. Everything had to go, including the mattress on the bed and the carpet. The Jacksons made a huge bonfire at the bottom of their garden and burnt everything, bit by bit.

Last of all, Mr Jackson brought out a big black refuse bag, full of all the feathers from the freezer. He was just about to throw it on the fire, when Julie saw it moving.

"Dad, drop it! It's still alive!" she cried. Her father dropped it instantly.

Battered and chewed, but still in one piece, Marmaduke crawled out of the top of the bag. Julie let out a howl of delight and swept him into her arms.

Mr Jackson bundled up the feathers again, and tossed them into the flames. Still hugging Marmaduke, Julie watched the feathers frizzle and curl in the heat. The wind sprang up and stirred the bonfire, disturbing a handful of small, downy feathers that had clumped together and fallen into the cooler embers.

"Burn," whispered Julie, "please burn."

As if to tease her, a capricious gust took hold of the feathers and lifted them skywards. Julie reached out to grab them with her free hand, but the wind was too quick for her. Swooping and diving, the ball of feathers escaped into the trees and beyond, as if they had taken on a whole new life of their own.

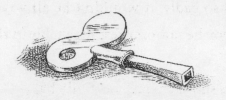

The Clockwork Dog

"It's quite simple," Richard's mother told him. "You can't have a dog. They're messy, they leave hair everywhere, they make the house smell, they take months to train and they chew the furniture. Why don't you settle for a cat or a hamster?"

"Because they're boring, you can't take them for walks and they're not good company," replied Richard sulkily.

It wasn't that his parents didn't like dogs, but his mother kept the house so neat and tidy that she was constantly in fear of anything making it messy.

On his birthday, Richard finally gave up hope. If his parents had got him the dog he'd wanted so badly, it wouldn't be all wrapped up in the box he saw on the coffee table in the living room.

"This should make you really happy!" cried his mother. Carefully, Richard took off the paper. Underneath was a plain cardboard box.

"We had to look a long time for this," grinned his father, rubbing his hands together in anticipation.

Richard tore the tape off the top of the box.

For one marvellous moment, Richard thought he had a real dog after all. He pulled it out of the box and put it on the floor. He stared at it. It was quite big, with silky black fur, sharp, pointed ears and a long, pointed snout. It didn't move.

"It's a *stuffed* dog!" he cried in disgust.

"Darling, it's a toy. A very special toy. We found it in a little shop just out of town," cried his mother in delight. She was so pleased they had been able to get him something he wanted. Almost.

"I think it's better than the real thing!" said his father encouragingly. He leaned over and picked up a large key from the bottom of the box. He placed it in a small hole in the side of the toy dog and turned it a few times.

"See? He winds up."

"Then what happens?" asked Richard, trying to decide whether or not to hide his disappointment for the sake of his parents.

"You pat him on the back, like this," grinned his father, demonstrating. The dog took a few steps forward and barked, the mechanism in its side whirring and clicking spasmodically.

"Hello," said the dog, in an electronic voice. "My name is Blackie, what's yours?"

"Richard," said Richard, before he could stop himself.

"That's a nice name," replied the dog. Its voice sounded like someone walking on gravel.

"But it doesn't *really* know my name," protested Richard. "I bet it would say the same thing to anyone."

"But don't you think it's fun?" asked his mother. "It says lots of other things too!"

"It's very nice," said Richard in a small voice. Privately, he thought it would be a better present for a five-year-old.

"Pity I can't take it for walks," he told his father.

"But you can! Look, there's a switch under his belly. If you push it the other way it doesn't talk, it just walks. Apparently, it's sensitive to pressure, so if you put a lead on and hold it back, it'll stop. Then, when you slacken the tension, it will start walking again, until it needs winding or you push the switch the other way."

So, it walked. Perhaps it wouldn't be so bad after all, decided Richard. It still wasn't as good as the real thing but at least it would be amusing to see what it could do.

The truth was, it couldn't do a lot. Sure, it walked just as his father said. It was even fun to take it to the park once or twice, then flick the switch that made it talk, just when someone came up to stroke it. But that was all there was to it.

Other than "What's your name?" and "That's a nice name," it could say "I'm hungry," which was equally useless, and "I need to go for a walk."

The toy dog went up considerably in Richard's estimation, when he took it into his classroom at school and his teacher tried to turn it out.

"Absolutely no pets allowed!" cried Mr Naylor. "Get it out of the room this minute!"

"But it's not a pet, sir," replied Richard, pushing the dog's backside to the floor so it would sit.

Mr Naylor strode down between the rows of desks until he stood, towering over Richard. Richard didn't have time to pat the dog on the back to make it talk, but Mr Naylor must have knocked it.

"Hello," said the dog. "My name is Blackie, what's yours?"

The whole class burst into fits of laughter at Mr Naylor's reaction — his feet *literally* left the ground when he heard the animal, it made him jump so badly.

When he managed to find his voice, Mr Naylor was madder than ever; he felt so dreadfully foolish.

"No toys allowed either, Richard!" he shouted. "Put that animal away."

With difficulty, Richard managed to squeeze Blackie into his school bag, but his head poked out of the top.

"That was so funny, Richard," whispered Jennifer, who sat behind him.

Richard looked around the room. Everyone was smiling at him except for one person. Winston.

Winston sat sullenly at his desk, right at the back of the class in the corner, glaring at Richard.

He was two years older than everyone else, so he was much bigger, but he had been kept down two classes because he didn't like learning. He thought it was a waste of time.

★ ★ ★ ★

At lunch, everyone wanted to have a look at Blackie. Richard knew the novelty wouldn't last long, but right now he was enjoying all the attention.

Suddenly, the crowd around him parted and went silent as Winston stepped forward.

"I want a word with you!" he snarled at Richard. Richard would have argued but Winston had a hold on his shirt collar, and was dragging him off to a corner of the school yard. Blackie trailed behind, pulling on the end of the lead.

"Right," said Winston, puffing his chest out, "I want that dog."

"I can't just give him away," protested Richard. "He was a birthday present."

"Tell your parents you lost him, then."

"No," said Richard flatly. Winston looked as if he was about to thump him, but thought better of it, because everyone was watching.

"OK, I'll buy him off you. How much do you want?"

"I'll have to ask my parents," said Richard, knowing he never would, but also knowing it would buy him some time. If Winston wanted something, he usually got it, one way or another.

Blackie, who had been lying on his side up to then, began to click and whirr again and climbed clumsily to his feet. Richard stared at him in surprise. The dog had a few tricks left.

"I want that dog," snapped Winston. Then abruptly, he turned and walked away. Richard breathed a sigh of relief. He decided never to bring Blackie into school again.

****

In his bedroom that night, Richard sat Blackie by the side of the bed. "You're more fun than I thought you would be," he told the toy. "But it's still a pity you're not real. It's also a pity I can't change your name to something more interesting."

★★★★

In the morning, Richard was woken by his mother's cries from the kitchen. "What is going on here?!" she screamed.

Richard ran to see what was wrong.

All over the floor were muddy footprints and the dustbin had been emptied EVERYWHERE. Richard had no idea the contents of the rubbish bin could cover such a large area. Every bit had been shredded and all the gooey stuff was stuck to everything.

"Don't tell me you let that toy we gave you walk in the mud!" Richard's mother demanded, pointing at the footprints.

"Of course not, Mum. I went straight to bed and stayed there. Besides, he couldn't have made all that mess with the rubbish."

"No, but you could have! Perhaps it was because we didn't get you a REAL dog! Even though that rotten toy cost the earth!"

"Mum, I promise I don't know anything about this," protested Richard. "Why would I make such a mess when you're bound to blame me?"

"This is just the sort of mess a real dog would make," sighed his mother. "That's why we didn't want one in the house."

"Perhaps a stray dog got in during the night?" suggested Richard.

"How? All the doors were locked."

"But I just saw the back door was open. I thought *you* must have opened it," said Richard.

A puzzled look crossed his mother's face as she went to check the door.

Through it, led a trail of mud.

****

"Right now, I'm glad you are a toy," Richard told Blackie, when he went back upstairs. The dog was sitting in the bedroom, staring straight ahead with his big brown glass eyes.

At school that day, Richard spent his time trying to avoid Winston, who kept tracking him down and asking, "When am I going to get my dog?"

When he got home, Blackie was still sitting in the bedroom, as he'd left him, staring straight ahead. Richard noticed how the dog's eyes seemed to follow him around the room.

He tried to ignore it because it made him feel uncomfortable. When he went to bed he pointed the dog towards the window.

But when he woke up in the morning, he opened his eyes to find Blackie staring straight at him. With a jolt, Richard sat up. The dog had turned its head! It was horrible, a life-like dog with a head turned right round so its nose was in line with its tail.

Gingerly, Richard took hold of Blackie's head and turned it back the right way. All sorts of cogs seemed to go off inside the animal, and it stood up and walked half-way across the room.

"I don't think I'll wind you up for a while," said Richard. But the dog carried on walking. Then it stopped suddenly, as the door swung open.

There stood Richard's mother, her face black as thunder.

"What is the meaning of this?" she demanded, shaking the piece of clothing she held in her hand. Richard took it from her and held it up. It was his absolutely favourite sweatshirt. At least it *was*, but now it was a dish-rag. Something had torn it to pieces.

"Oh, no!" he cried. "What happened to it?"

"I thought you could tell me that!" retorted his mother. "I was just about to put it in the wash when I discovered what sort of state you'd left it in."

"But I didn't, I didn't! Honestly!" protested Richard. "Why would I tear up my favourite sweatshirt? I bet it was done by whatever got into the kitchen the other night."

Richard's mother stormed out. "You're not getting another!" she snapped over her shoulder.

Richard couldn't help himself — tears rolled down his face. He was stopped by the sound of a metallic laugh.

But since it couldn't have been the toy dog, Richard decided it must have been his imagination…

****

While Richard was sitting at his desk, waiting for his first class to start, Winston called across the room. "Don't forget we have a deal!"

"What does he mean?" asked Jennifer from the desk behind.

"He wants my toy dog," replied Richard in a

low voice. "He thinks I'm going to sell it to him, but I haven't said I will."

"Oh yeah," sighed Jennifer, "if he's decided you're going to sell it, then I guess you'll probably end up having to. You know how nasty he is if he doesn't get what he wants. He could make your life very difficult."

"It already is," Richard told her. "It's the toy," he explained. "It's SO real that it's beginning to make me nervous. On top of that, a stray dog or something got into the house and messed it up. Now my parents are blaming me."

"You don't think your toy did it, do you?" laughed Jennifer.

Richard said he didn't think so. It was just that everything was going wrong at the same time.

Jennifer walked home with him to have another look at Blackie. But Blackie wasn't where Richard had left him in the bedroom. He wasn't there at all.

"Look at your room!" exclaimed Jennifer. "Do you usually keep it like this?"

Richard stared in horror. All his books had been pulled off the shelves and the pages were torn out, half his clothes were ripped to pieces, what was left of his football lay in small pieces all over the floor, and his bed had been stripped and the sheets were covered in mud.

He sank on to the bed in despair. "It's never like this!" he wailed.

Jennifer stared at the walls. "There are scratch marks all over your paintwork," she observed.

"We have to be quick," said Richard suddenly. "If I don't get this cleaned up, Mum will think I've done it!"

"I bet that's what you say to everyone when you want someone to help you tidy your room!" laughed Jennifer.

"I didn't do this," he said quietly.

Jennifer's smile vanished. "You're serious, aren't you?" she said in surprise.

"Very," replied Richard, grabbing a carrier bag and stuffing all the little bits of football into it.

When the room was as tidy as they could get it, they went to find Blackie.

"But I thought he was still in your room," Richard's mother told him. "Does Jennifer want to stay for supper?"

"Er... yes," said Richard absent-mindedly, leading Jennifer off to find his father.

"No, I haven't seen that toy dog since you last had him downstairs," his father informed him.

Richard took Jennifer aside. "My parents have no reason to lie," he said. "There's no way anything could have got into my room today, or Mum would have seen it. The only thing that has been in my room, apart from me, is that rotten toy. Now what do you think?"

"I think we're both going crazy," whispered Jennifer, "because I think we both think the toy did it."

"So where is it?" Richard wanted to know. "We have to find it before it does any more damage."

****

They finally discovered Blackie in the garden shed.

"How did he get out here?" cried Jennifer.

"I think it's a pretty good bet that he walked on his own," replied Richard. "Now we have to get him inside."

"Are you going to carry him?"

Richard realised he didn't want to touch the toy. Blackie was staring up at him glassily, his head at an angle, even though he wasn't supposed to be programmed to be able to turn it that way.

Then he blinked.

"Did you see that?" gasped Jennifer. "He looks so weird. He looks more real than when you brought him into school, but his shape isn't quite right, if you know what I mean."

Carefully, Richard picked Blackie up and carried him inside at arm's length.

"Open the lid to the toy box in the corner," he told Jennifer, when they were back in his room.

He was just about to put the dog inside when he had a second thought. "We should make sure he's wound right down first," he decided.

Out in the garden, they walked the dog round and round until its mechanism creaked and groaned and the whirring noise that accompanied every step, stopped. The dog came to a grinding halt.

"Now," announced Richard, "we can put him away."

They stowed him in the toy chest, fastening the latch that held the lid down.

****

Richard woke the next morning, stretched and yawned and glanced towards the toy chest. Suddenly, he got an awful squirmy feeling, as if someone had slipped a wet eel down his back. The lid of the toy chest was hanging off its hinges!

Why hadn't he heard anything during the night? In a panic, he searched the room, then the house – but he couldn't find the dog.

His parents were calling for him from the kitchen, arms folded and furious expressions. Across the floor were spread the contents of the fridge. The spilt milk, overturned dishes of leftover stew, half-chewed vegetables, tooth-punctured orange cartons and mashed cheese, were all evidence that Blackie had been there.

"We think you have a problem," announced Richard's mother.

"We think you're doing all this to draw our attention to the fact we won't get you a real dog," said his father.

"But I didn't do this!" protested Richard.

"Well, who else could have done it?" asked his mother. "I have to tell you this is not the way to get what you want. Now, clean up this mess."

Richard was late for school that morning. First, Mr Naylor told him off. Then Winston found him, demanding the dog again.

"He got out of the toy chest," Richard told Jennifer later. "If I can find him when I get home, I'm going to give him to Winston."

"I think we should try and get rid of him in a more permanent way," said Jennifer quietly.

****

When they got back to Richard's that afternoon, they discovered Blackie in a bush at the bottom of the garden.

"I don't want to touch him," admitted Richard sheepishly.

"I'll get him out," offered Jennifer. She reached into the bush but pulled her hands out quickly when Blackie let out a mechanical growl.

"How could he get here when he wasn't wound up?" asked Richard.

"Maybe because he wound himself up?"

suggested Jennifer, pointing to the large key that was sticking out of Blackie's side.

"But I put the key in one of my bedroom drawers," Richard told her.

"My name is Blackie," said the dog, its bottom jaw moving up and down mechanically. "What's yours?"

"Shut up," snapped Richard.

"That's a nice name," said the dog.

Richard reached into the bush, grabbed Blackie by the scruff of his neck and hauled him out on to the lawn. The dog's legs whirred and kicked uselessly, then stopped, as if it was thinking of what to do next. Then it raised its head and clambered to its feet.

All Jennifer could do was stare. "If I wasn't sure you were telling the truth before, I am now," she breathed.

The dog let out a single mechanical laugh and began to plod steadily towards the house. Richard ran to the garden shed, found an old plastic bin and upended it over the toy. There were loud scratching sounds as Blackie tried to escape.

"Quick, sit on this!" Richard told Jennifer. While she was sitting on the bin, Richard took a spade and began to dig a deep hole just behind the garden shed. He worked very fast.

"I think the dog is going to scratch his way out through the plastic!" Jennifer called.

Richard worked furiously. When he thought the hole was deep enough, he and Jennifer pulled the bin, with Blackie rolling around on the ground inside, towards it until the bin was actually over the hole.

Then they pulled the bin away, and there, at the bottom of the pit, lay Blackie, kicking and growling.

Richard took the shovel and started to fill the hole in as quickly as he could. Finally, he finished it off by jumping up and down on the heap of earth, until Jennifer had to stop him.

"I don't think he'll get out of there," she told him.

It was wonderful, for two days Richard went round grinning. Even Winston asked him why he was so happy.

"No reason," Richard told him.

"So, where's my dog?" demanded Winston.

"I couldn't sell it to you even if I wanted to," replied Richard, "because someone stole it."

"I don't believe you," snarled Winston, threateningly.

****

But then on the evening of the second day, Richard was woken by a scratching at his bedroom door. With the hair standing up on the back of his neck, he got out of bed, turned on the light and opened the door a tiny crack.

It was Blackie, covered in mud. The dog let out another single laugh. "My name is Blackie, what's yours?"

Richard shut the door quietly. But wait, what if Blackie tore the house apart? Should he let the dog in, or risk shutting him out? Either way, the choice wasn't easy.

Hurriedly, Richard rifled through his bedroom cupboard until he found what he was looking for. It was an old travel bag.

Opening the door again, he found Blackie still standing on the landing. As the dog began to move towards the bedroom, Richard pounced, throwing the bag over his head and trapping him. Then he closed the bag and zipped it up.

He stayed awake the rest of the night making sure Blackie didn't escape, and spending most of the time trying to brush up the trail of mud that Blackie had left behind him. Hopefully, his mother wouldn't notice because the carpet was brown...

At breakfast, he took the bag downstairs and put it on the kitchen table. Blackie never seemed to move when his parents were present, so he thought it was safe to leave him there.

"What are you doing with that?" asked his mother curiously.

"Oh, it's just some old toys, I said I'd lend them to someone at school for their little brother," replied Richard, thinking fast.

****

At school, he found Winston.

"OK, you wanted it," Richard announced. "Well, he's all yours."

"You should have made him pay you something," whispered Jennifer.

Winston opened up the bag. "Yuk, it's all dirty. I don't want this!"

"That's why I'm not charging you anything," grinned Richard. "He's yours for nothing. But you have to clean him up."

"Does he still work?"

"Of course he does," smiled Richard, reassuringly. "I've left the wind-up key in his side for you. There's only one condition: my parents mustn't know I've given him to you, so don't bring him to school or someone might tell them."

Winston nodded his big head stupidly and walked off with a wide grin on his face. Richard walked away with an even bigger grin.

"We may have finally got rid of Blackie!" he told Jennifer, trying to shake off the feeling of unease that still troubled him.

****

But the days went by and nothing happened except for a change in Winston. First, he got more bad tempered, then he grew quieter and then he became nervous. The slightest noise made him jump. He sat in his corner of the classroom, not speaking even when spoken to. He looked preoccupied, and wherever he was, he kept one eye on the door.

"How's the dog?" asked Richard one day. Winston nearly leapt out of his skin.

"Fine," he replied abruptly. Then he hesitated. "Tell me," he asked Richard almost timidly, "did the dog do anything... well... strange, when you had it?"

"No," lied Richard.

Jennifer walked up to them. "Anything wrong with the toy?" she asked innocently.

Winston shook his head. "I'm not sure," he replied, hesitantly. "Richard, would you like your dog back?"

"No! He's yours now," said Richard firmly.

* * * *

That was the day Richard had a surprise when his father got home from work.

His parents called him down from his room — and there it was! Sitting in the kitchen, waiting for him.

For a moment Richard froze. It was black, big, and had huge brown eyes and a long nose.

His mother looked at him expectantly. "Well, what do you think?" she asked him, her eyes shining.

The dog stood up and walked towards him, its tongue hanging out, wet with drool.

"He's REAL!" gasped Richard. His parents looked at each other and grinned.

"We had a long talk with a dog breeder," explained his father. "It seems your mother and I had been worried about nothing. A puppy is difficult and destructive sometimes, but a well-trained dog like this is fine, as long as it gets plenty of exercise and care and doesn't get bored."

"Fred is here on a month's trial," added Richard's mother. "His owner is going abroad, so he needs a good home. But if you can't take proper care of him, the owner will find someone else who can. Now, I think we should plan on buying him a few toys tomorrow, what do you think?"

"I think he's the most wonderful present I've ever had!" cried Richard, hugging both his parents. Fred followed Richard up to his room as if he knew the way.

When Richard woke in the morning, it was Fred who stared at him with big eyes and a sloppy wet tongue, whimpering to be taken for a walk.

★★★★

The next day, being Saturday, Richard and his mother took Fred shopping. His owner had given them a lead, a collar and a dog basket, but Fred had no real toys of his own.

They got home with a bag of bits and pieces they'd chosen, but none of which Fred appeared to find interesting.

"I don't know what he wants," complained Richard. "He just doesn't seem to want to look at anything." He bounced a small red ball in front of Fred's face, but Fred just stretched out on the floor and yawned widely.

Richard waved a rubber bone at him, then tossed it across the room. "Fetch!" he cried, but Fred wasn't interested.

Jennifer called round to see them both, but she didn't have any luck, either.

"Perhaps he's just a boring dog?" she suggested. "Look on the bright side, you could still have Blackie."

* * * *

On Monday, Winston didn't come to school. Instead his father dropped in on his way to work to tell Mr Naylor his son was ill.

"I'm beginning to think we should rescue Winston from Blackie," Jennifer told Richard, "because I'm sure Blackie is the real reason why Winston is staying away. Perhaps we can come up with an idea that will get rid of the dog once and for all?"

Richard didn't know what to do. He felt guilty that Winston was being taught a lesson by the horrible toy, but the idea of having anything to do with the dog again, terrified him.

* * * *

When he got home, he discovered he didn't have a choice. Blackie was sitting on the doorstep, waiting for him. He must have been through quite a lot since Richard last saw him, because his fake fur was matted and filthy, one of his legs was very bent, half of an ear was missing and his tail had two kinks in it. Richard guessed that Winston had tried to get rid of him a few times, too...

Slowly, he reached over the dog's head and opened the door. Blackie didn't move, but his eyes never left Richard.

Carefully, Richard raised one leg, then the other and stepped over the animal.

He found his mother in the living room, reading the paper.

"Do you know Blackie is sitting on the doorstep?" he asked her.

She looked up in surprise. "Why, no dear. What's he doing there? I thought you must have put him away now you have Fred, who, by the way, insisted on waiting for you in your bedroom. He seems to like it there."

"Er, Mum, I'm going to leave Blackie on the doorstep for now. I'll fetch him later," muttered Richard, hurrying out of the room.

Fred jumped to his feet as soon as he saw Richard. His tail wagged furiously and he panted excitedly. Richard threw his arms around the dog's neck.

"I'm just popping next door for a few minutes," Richard's mother called up the stairs. He heard her shut the front door behind her and his heart sank. Now she was gone, Blackie would move.

He heard the grating of teeth on the handle of the front door followed by a short silence. Then there was a shuffle, thump, shuffle noise on the stairs, followed by another short silence.

Richard's bedroom door swung open and there stood his old toy. "I've... come... home," Blackie's voice grated. "Winston... is... no... fun."

Fred was having a strange reaction to the toy dog. He cocked his head first one way, then the other, listening.

Without taking his eyes off Blackie, Richard reached out and took hold of the cricket bat his grandfather gave him two Christmases ago. It had never been used, but now it was going to be *very* useful.

Blackie moved forward with a limping motion because of his bent leg; his mechanism sounded rusty and grating.

Suddenly, Fred bounded forward. He took hold of Blackie by one of his ears and dragged him into the centre of the room.

Blackie lost his balance and fell over. Fred sniffed and prodded him and Blackie's mechanism hissed and growled in protest, the clockwork legs kicking uselessly.

Fred bit into Blackie's leg, and swung him into the air, beating him onto the floor again and again. Then he dropped him and waited. Blackie let out a slow snarl.

So Fred picked him up and beat him on the floor some more. All Richard could do was watch in amazement.

A split opened up in Blackie's side and

stuffing began to fly out all over the room. Fred shook Blackie from side to side and a cog shot past Richard's ear and hit the wall behind him.

"No one heard me knock, but your front door was open so I came in," said Jennifer from the doorway. "I came to see what you want to do about Blackie—"

Fred stopped just long enough to look at her and return to what he was doing.

"My… name… is…" said a metallic voice from inside Blackie. Fred was greatly encouraged by this and began to dig at the hole in Blackie's side to see where the noise came from. His nose emerged, covered in fluff. In his teeth was the small plastic box that held Blackie's voice.

"…Blackie," said the box. Then the tone got higher. "Put… me… down…" squawked the box.

Richard and Jennifer shuddered. Fred looked at Richard through the threads of floating stuffing.

Richard could have sworn Fred smiled, just before he sank his teeth into the plastic box so it crunched and was silent. Then he dropped it on the floor and stared up at Richard, wagging his tail as though he'd done something terribly clever.

Jennifer looked at Blackie's unstuffed shape lying at Fred's feet, and at the little bits and pieces of Blackie that lay around the room. Then she began to laugh.

"You finally found a toy for the dog!" she shrieked.

Fred picked up Blackie's limp, woolly coat and carried it to the dog basket in the corner. Now it looked like nothing more threatening than an empty cushion cover.

Richard's mother peered into the room. "I could hear all the commotion from next door," she protested, her voice dying away as she saw the mess in front of her.

"It's all right, Mum, we've been playing with the dog," said Richard, trying to control the hysterical feeling that was creeping up inside him. It began bubbling and grew and grew until he was rolling around on the bed laughing and holding his sides, with tears running down his face.

"We've been playing with the dog!" Richard cried out again, laughing so much it hurt. Jennifer quietened down just long enough to assure Richard's mother that they would clean the room up, then she looked at Fred sitting on what was left of Blackie and burst into peals of laughter again.

It was a day or so before Winston returned to school, and not much longer before he tried to return to his old ways.

Richard and Jennifer caught Winston telling one of the small boys that he would have to give him his lunch money. Richard walked up to Winston and looked him in the eye. "My name is Blackie," he said quietly, "what's yours?"

Winston went white. He told the small boy to forget about the lunch money, and slunk away.

It became a school saying. No one knew why it worked, but every time Winston tried to bully someone and they said, "My name is Blackie, what's yours?" he would stop what he was doing and leave, until finally, he never bothered anyone again.

And whenever Richard or Jennifer heard it, they collapsed in heaps of helpless laughter. No one at school could understand it. So they kept saying it, anyway.

****

Not far away, on the city tip, the rats scuttled, searching for food.

"I belong," said a disjointed mechanical voice from beneath the huge mounds of household garbage and rotting matter, "to Number Ten, Watkins Street. Please take me home. I belong to Number Ten, Watkins Street. Please take me home. I belong… I belong… I belong. Take me home."

The old man's gnarled and bony brown hand reached down into the piles of rubbish, pulling and tugging overstuffed and torn plastic refuse sacks out of the way, until he found what he was looking for. His hand emerged holding a small, battered black box.

"Hello, my name... Blackie, what's yours?" said the box.

The skinny old tramp grinned widely. He slipped the little box into his pocket. He was sure he could find a use for it...